D0529721

No more icy blasts or creaking joints. No more frozen combs or frost-bitten toes. Now new sounds come from the boards, beams, and thawing arms of the winter barn.

With that first sip the world relaxes.

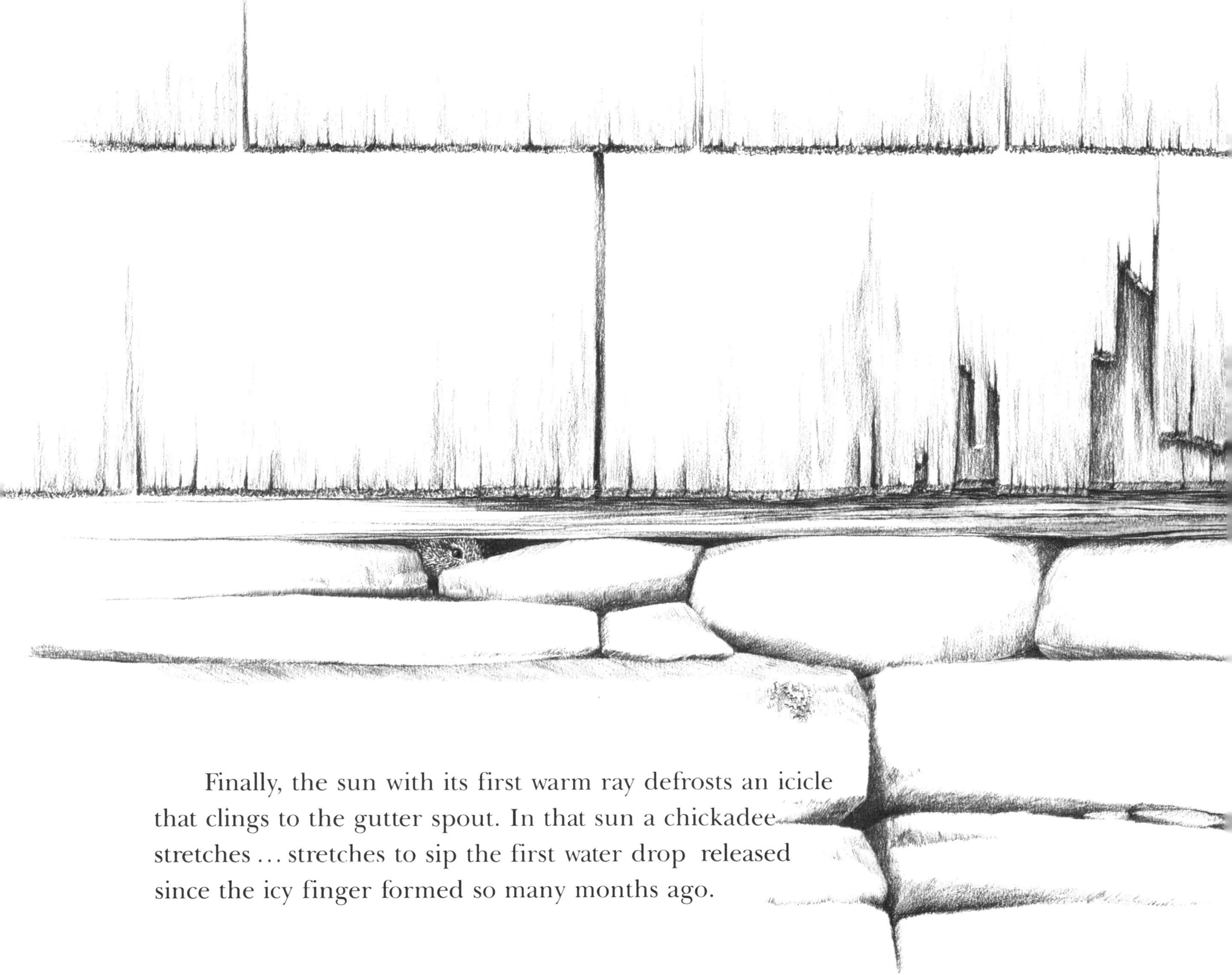

Finally, the sun with its first warm ray defrosts an icicle that clings to the gutter spout. In that sun a chickadee stretches ... stretches to sip the first water drop released since the icy finger formed so many months ago.

Chickens sitting on the backs of sheep warm their naked legs and feet, waiting through endless hours of frosty, lung-burning nights for the late winter sun to arrive.

Deepest in the hay, unknown to all but the bravest of cats, sleeps coon. She uses up her summer-stored fat and waits for the day when her young are born and can be led down to the dishes of food reserved for those more domestic.

High up where the wild cat hides, there are mortises and tenons, great sockets that hold together the barn's huge bones. Stretched and pulled over the years, they have gaps. Gaps where bats sleep winter away. In summer they fly forth when evening approaches, feasting on mosquitoes, flies, and pests of all kinds. They help the martin and swallow remove black flies and gnats from the barn's summer sky. At the first snap of cold they slow. They search out a winter lair under shingles, deep in piles of wood, in any crevice or hole large enough for two, crowding together for their long sleep. So, too, do carpenter ants gather within their catacombs of wood, waiting for a warmer day. Winter is a time for huddling, crowding, and taking small breaths.

Some are fugitives from the forest who enter the arms of the winter barn to escape the furious predators of the wild: the bobcat, the fisher, the great horned owl, and the unforgiving, killing cold. Wild kitties, great rugged things, enter all brazen and hard, only to cower high in the loft at the slightest sound while they study the order of things below. Some otherwise quarrelsome creatures make peace in the face of a common enemy: cold. Gradually they find their place among cats, skunk, horses, chickens, and sheep. No home for bullies. No place for quarrels. Only pleasant ones survive. There are too many allies.

Most of the cats belong to the barn. They know the warmest lairs, and they know when ice will be chopped from horses' trough. Twice a day they steal a sip. Quickly … quickly … or new ice will steal the chance!

Skunk lies there, too. She sleeps by day between two beams underneath a horse's feet and, when darkness falls, ambles forth to seek her evening meal … upstairs. She has a hole through which she climbs to the domestic floor above, the floor of horses, sheep, chickens, and cats … and cats! Fourteen cats weather winter here: cats in hay, cats in barrels, cats in boxes, and cats in cats. Kitty food suits skunk just fine!

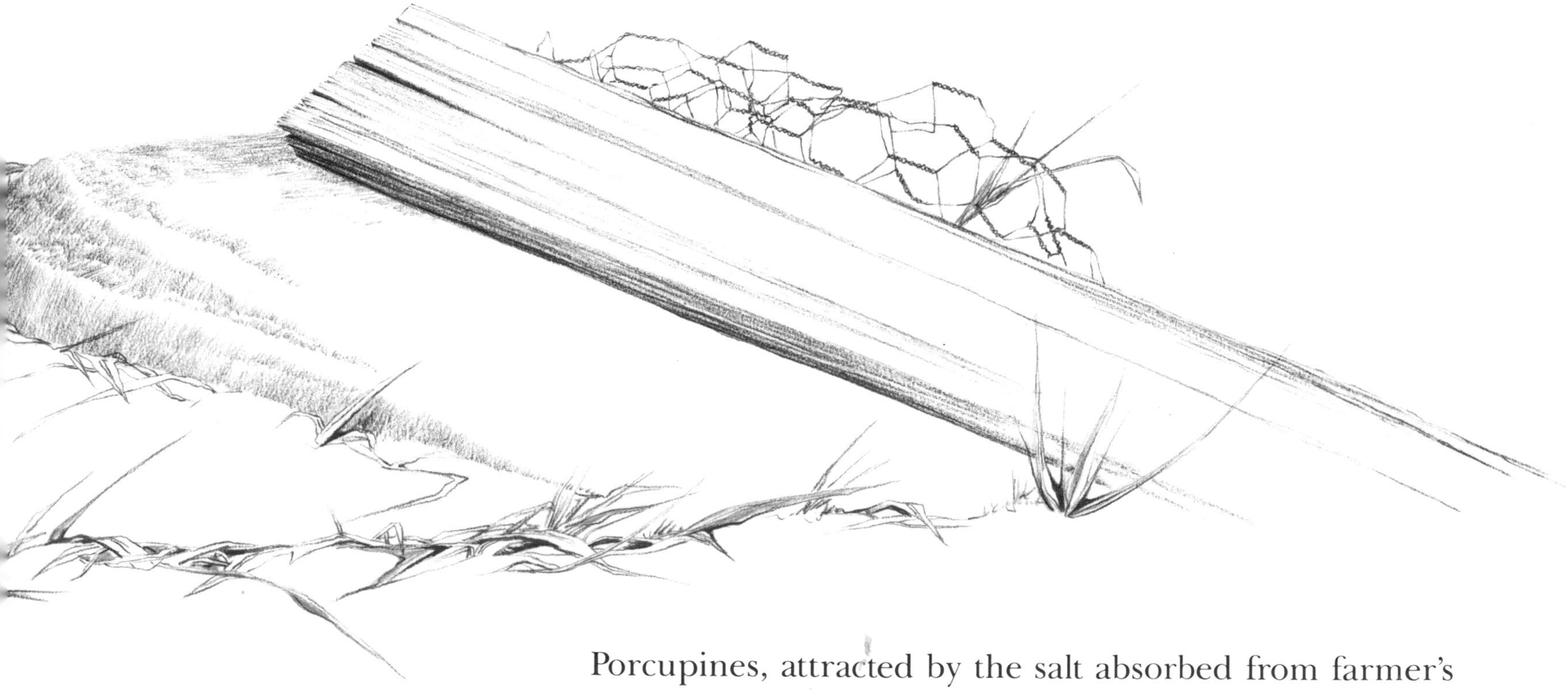

Porcupines, attracted by the salt absorbed from farmer's hands into the handles of ancient tools, nestle in a pile of long-forgotten, rotten hay.

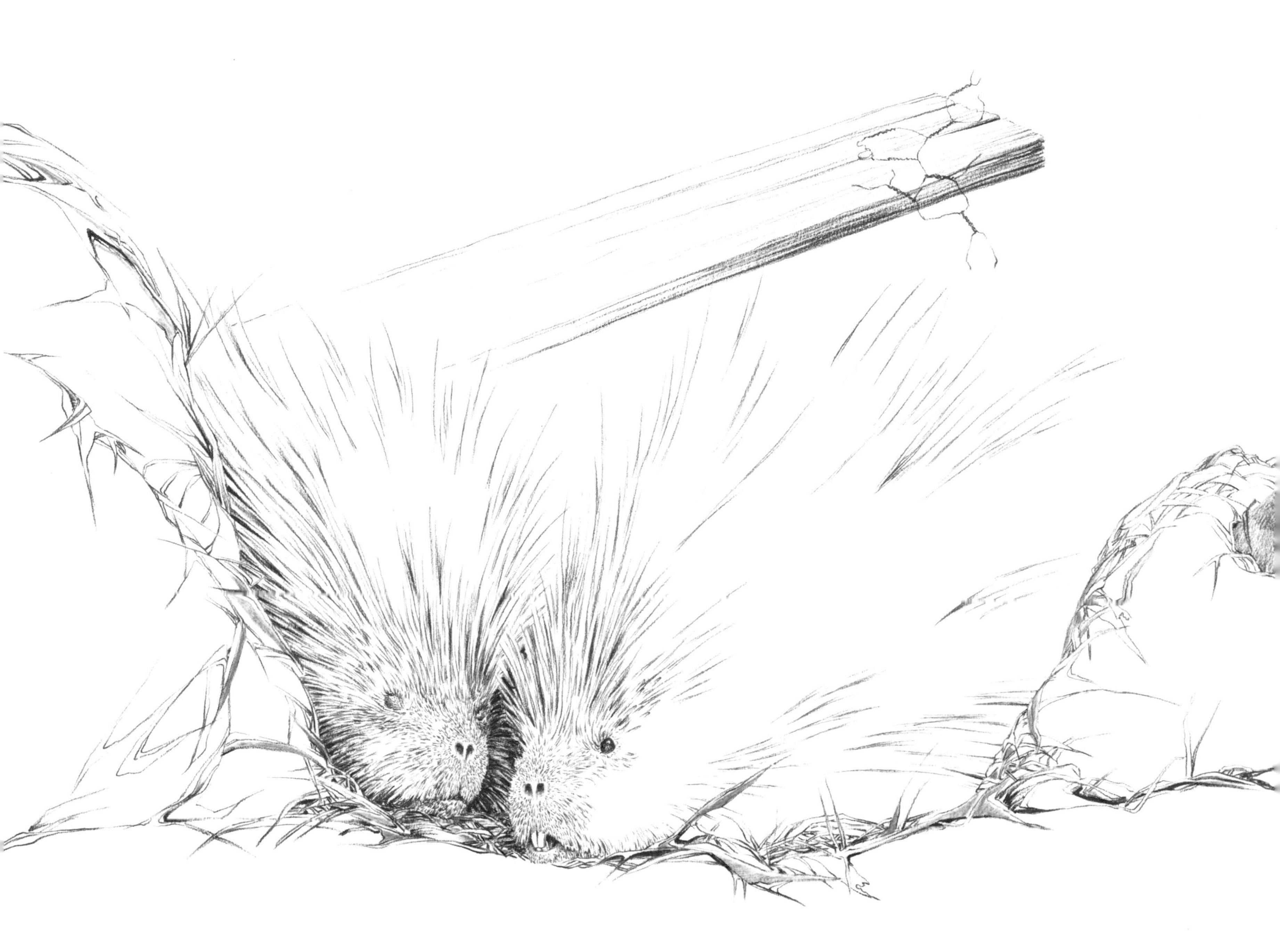

They wait and share warm spaces. Now no quarrels over private places. Now all share to survive. Beneath the barn sleep woodchucks in a burrow of their own design, with an entrance between two stones that dog could never move.

Some days a treat of turkey grower spills ... or cat food ... or, best of all, the salty seaweed vitamin usually reserved for horse or dog. For mouse a winter barn is an easy place, a place whose tunnels and hidden entries protect him from the cats and hawks of summer, and where he finds a banquet at his feet demanding no risks, no discomforts so common in the wild.

As the cold grows deeper, the winter barn becomes the core of life in the thick, white world. Snow drifts down. Day after day it falls till beams groan and grumble with the added weight on the great dripping marshmallow of a barn. Tons of snow condense the life within.

The creatures wait.

Escape.

There are red-ant nests in crevices packed with vegetable bits, and, when frosty days begin to nip, white-footed mice invade the underparts of the barn, abandoning their outdoor, fair-weather homes for the safety of deep runways, passages that lead under the grain-room floor, where a knothole in an old cracked board has been a friend to the offspring of many generations. From year to year they remember. They remember molasses, alfalfa meal, oats, cracked corn, and the feed-bag strings left hanging in the great steel drums by the owner of the barn.

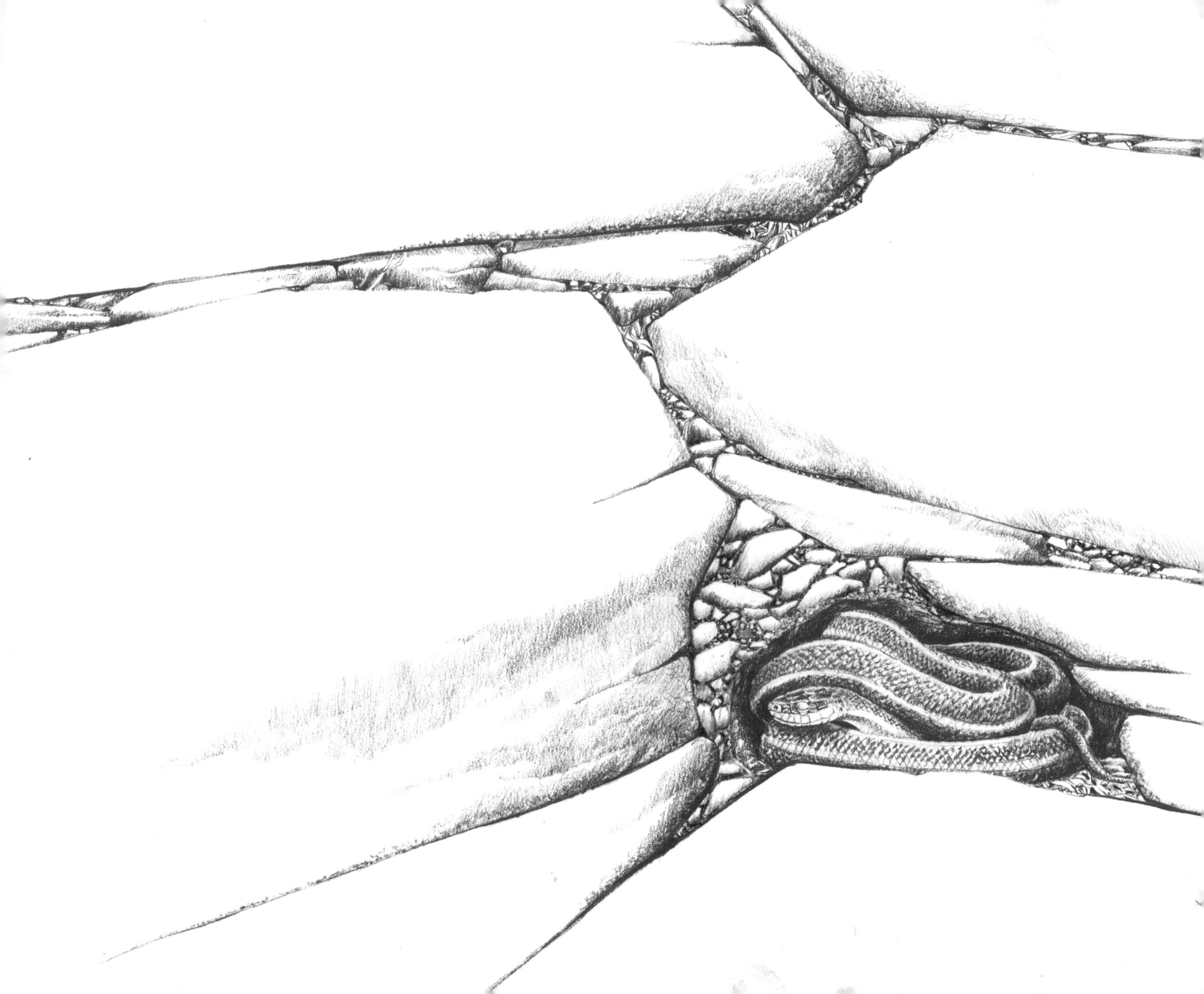

To most of its creatures the barn is the world, for inside those walls their comforts lie and their safety is assured. One who sleeps deep within grass-filled spaces, between and under tons of stone, is a ribbon snake. There he lies, safe from the killing air, waiting for warming stones of spring to tell his blood it is time to stir and sun himself awake for summer.

A Hessian soldier laid these rocks. A man left over from another's war grappled with the stones, laying a foundation more solid than one of any modern steel or concrete. A massive puzzle, the granite maze protects within its depths any creature fortunate enough to fit.

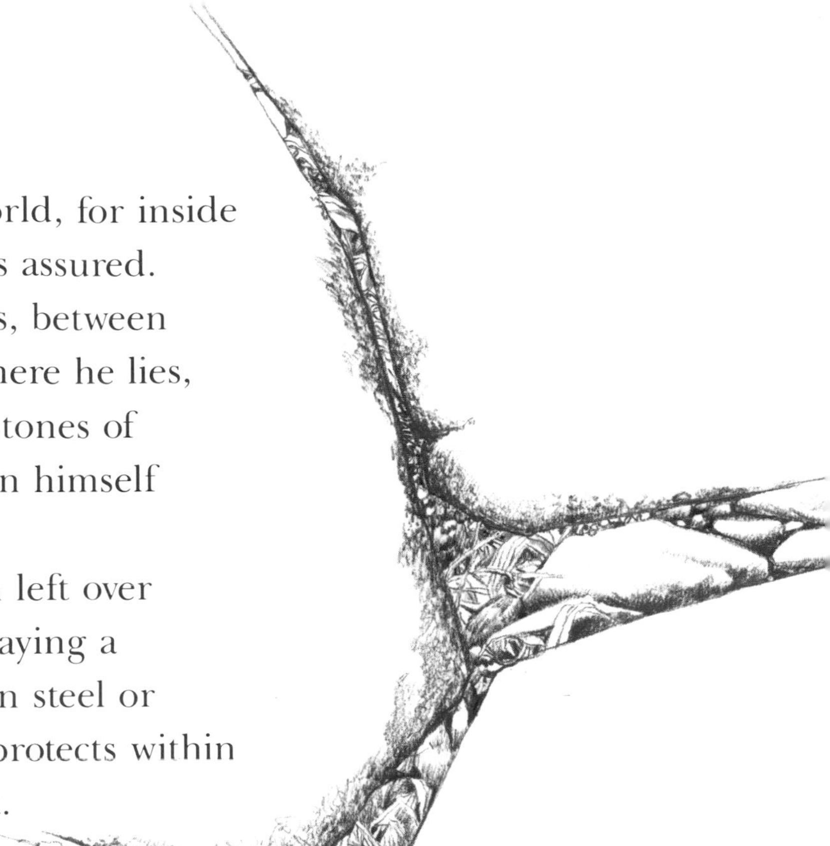

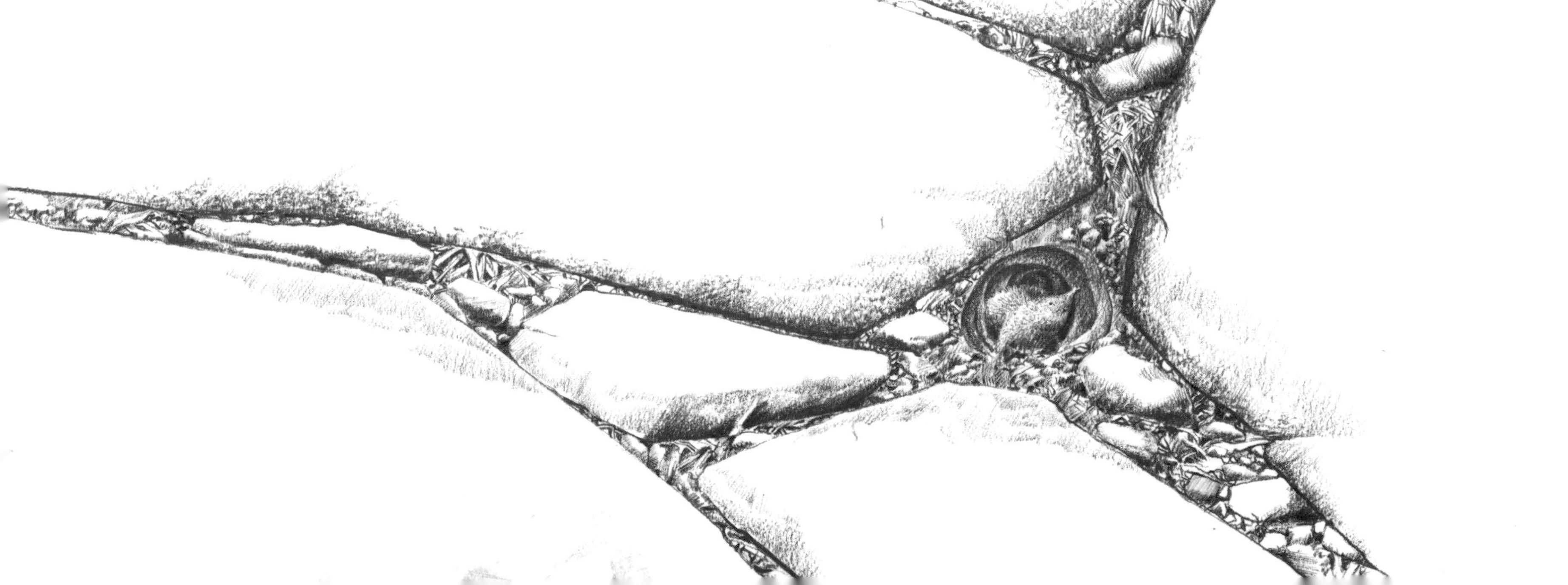

Like a great woolly mammoth frozen in the Arctic ice, the winter barn waits, locked in a vast white landscape in Maine. At thirty below, with each icy breeze that darts through cracks and holes, wooden fibers wince and complain. They creak. They crackle. They play their own music, those great oak beams hewn two hundred years ago.

Oak beams, hemlock boards, and cedar shingles, linked together with pegs and nails, form a giant crystal chandelier in winter. The barn sings its own songs about winter, summer, and the lives held safe within the great dark cloak of hand-hewn wood.

To Tracy
and all the creatures
in our winter barn

Macmillan Publishing Company, 866 Third Avenue, New York, NY 10022. Collier Macmillan Canada, Inc.

First edition Printed in the United States of America 10 9 8 7 6 5 4 3 2 1

The text of this book is set in 14 pt. Baskerville. The illustrations are rendered in charcoal and wash.

Library of Congress Cataloging-in-Publication Data

Parnall, Peter. Winter barn. Summary: A dilapidated old barn shelters a wide variety of animals, including snakes, porcupines, cats, and a skunk, during the sub-zero winter temperatures of Maine, while they wait for the first signs of spring. 1. Animals—Juvenile fiction. [1. Winter—Fiction. 2. Animals—Fiction. 3. Barns—Fiction] I. Title. PZ10.3.P228Wi 1986 [Fic] 85-23898 ISBN 0-02-770170-0

WINTER BARN

WRITTEN AND ILLUSTRATED BY PETER PARNALL

Macmillan Publishing Company New York

Collier Macmillan Publishers London

WINTER BARN